The Clumsies

make a mess

of the BIG show

First published in paperback in Great Britain by HarperCollins *Children's Books*
2011

HarperCollins *Children's Books* is a division of HarperCollins*Publishers* Ltd
77-85 Fulham Palace Road, Hammersmith, London W6 8JB

Visit us on the web at www.harpercollins.co.uk

1

Text copyright © Sorrel Anderson 2011
Illustrations copyright © Nicola Slater 2011

ISBN: 978-0-00-733936-5

BY SORREL ANDERSON

Illustrated by Nicola Slater

The Clumsies

make a mess of the BIG show

For Sausage

The Clumsies also make a mess in:

The Clumsies Make a Mess

The Clumsies Make a Mess Of
the Seaside

Contents

Trolley

t was a Tuesday morning and the Clumsies were enjoying their breakfast when the door crashed open and Howard staggered in, muttering.

'*Extraordinary,*' he muttered.

'What is?' asked Purvis.

'Must have gone mad,' he muttered.

'Who must?' asked Purvis.

'It's over,' he muttered, 'and I should know, I had to work right through it. We don't need one now. Especially not one that looks like that.'

'Gentggggdgng gggtggggddggt?' said Mickey Thompson, with his mouth full of banana.

'Eh?' said Howard.

'He said what don't we need one of that looks like what?' explained Purvis.

'**Ygsh,**' confirmed Mickey Thompson.

'**Tut,**' said Howard. 'Don't speak with your mouth full, Mickey Thompson.'

'**Shggyg,**' said Mickey Thompson, adding a spoonful of egg.

'So what is it we don't we need one of that looks like something?' asked Purvis.

'A Christmas tree,' said Howard. 'It's the middle of January! The time for Christmas trees has been and gone, but Mr Bullerton's just put one up in the foyer."

'**Whosha ggmshgggmshgg?**' crunched Mickey Thompson.

'What did I just say?' said Howard, brushing toast crumbs off his face.

'**G-gumf,**' swallowed Mickey Thompson.

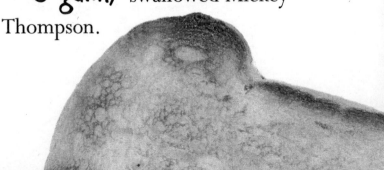

'What's a Christmas tree?'

'Well... you know,' said Howard.

'No, we don't,' said the mice.

'Well, it's... it's...' Howard fluttered his hands up and down. The mice stared at him, uncomprehendingly.

'It's a tree,' said Howard. 'That you have at Christmas time.'

The mice stared at him, baffledly.

'And you decorate it with lights and stars and fairies and stuff,' said Howard.

Purvis and Mickey Thompson started bouncing and squeaking.

'And then you take it down again,' said Howard, 'which is part of the point. Stop that – it goes right through my head.'

'Can you take us to see it?' said Mickey Thompson. 'Can you? Can you?'

'I expect so,' sighed Howard. 'As long as you're quiet.'

'When?' said Purvis. 'Wh— Oh!'

'What?' said Howard.

'Post!' said Purvis, and the Clumsies dived under the desk. There was a clacketty, rattley noise

out in the corridor and the
postman arrived, pushing a trolley
piled high with post.

'Delivery for Howard
Armitage!' announced the
postman, coming in with a large
box. 'It's work. From Mr
Bullerton.'

'Marvellous,' said Howard.

'He said to say you're to do it
straight away.'

'Wonderful,' said Howard.

'It gets better,' said the
postman, going out and coming in
again with another large box. And
another. And another.
And another.

Trolley

'Done something to upset his highness?' asked the postman, cheerfully.

'Very probably,' said Howard.

'Behaving strangely, he is,' said the postman, 'what with the tree and everything. It's the complaints, you know.'

'Err, what is?' said Howard.

'People have been complaining about him making them work all through Christmas,' said the postman, 'and he hasn't taken it well. Come to think of it, Howard, he hasn't been right since

that conference you went on
together.'

'Hmm,' said Howard, guiltily.

'Cup
of
tea?'

'Don't mind if I do,' said the
postman. 'Got a thirst on, all those
boxes.'

'Bother,' *whispered* Mickey
Thompson, to Purvis. 'If he's stuck
doing all that work he won't have
time to take us to see the tree.'

'We'll just have to go by
ourselves then, won't we?'
whispered Purvis. 'Come on.'

'What, now?' **squeaked**
Mickey Thompson. 'We can't go
now.'

'Why can't we?' said Purvis,
starting to tiptoe out.

'Err, err, Ortrud's asleep,' said
Mickey Thompson.

'Well, that's OK. We can take
her to see it another time,' said

Purvis. 'Come on! Let's go!'

'I don't want to,' said Mickey Thompson.

'Yes, you do,' said Purvis. 'You said you did, before.'

'And now I don't.'

'Why ever not?'

'Oh, no reason,' said Mickey Thompson, trying to sound casual.

Purvis advanced on Mickey Thompson and there was a small scuffle.

'*Gerroff!*' said
Mickey Thompson, **'*All right.*'**

'Tell me,' said Purvis.

'It,' whispered Mickey Thompson,
and pointed towards the corridor.

'What it?' asked Purvis.

'That… post trolley. It's…
there.'

'Oh, don't be so soft,' said
Purvis. 'Come along.' And he led the
way into the corridor, where the
trolley was waiting. It was wooden
and big, with wheels and shelves,
and it was saying something.

'**TEN TWENTY ONE**,' it said.
'**TEN TWENTY TWO.**'

'Hello,' said Purvis.
CLACK! rattled the trolley.

'*Eep,*' said Mickey Thompson, ducking behind Purvis.

'Ten twenty seven.'

'What is?' asked Purvis.

'The amount I'm behind schedule,' said the trolley.

'Ah,' said Purvis. 'I see.'

'**TEN THIRTY THREE.** What are they doing in there?'

'Having a cup of tea,' said Purvis.

CLATTER! went the trolley.

'Because of the boxes,' Purvis explained.

'Forty *one*!' said the trolley, tetchily. 'Four five six seven nine.'

'I think you might be speeding up a little,' said Purvis.

CLACK! went the trolley, juddering. 'I'M NOT THE ONLY ONE, **FIFTY TWO**: LOOK WHO'S COMING.'

It was Mr Bullerton, Howard's boss, steaming up the corridor towards them.

'Eeeeep!' went the mice, darting under the trolley just in time as Mr Bullerton arrived.

CLATTER! went the trolley, as Mr Bullerton kicked it. **'WHAT'S THIS THING DOING OUT HERE?'** he bellowed.

CLATTER!

went the cups, as Mr Bullerton
entered Howard's room, where
Howard and the postman were
drinking tea.

'AND WHAT'S
GOING ON IN
HERE? Or NOT, to be
precise. Well?'

'Oh, ah,' said Howard. 'Mr
Bullerton! We were just… err…'

'Having a cup of tea?' suggested
Mr Bullerton.

'Exactly,' said Howard.

'How nice,' said Mr Bullerton, kicking one of the boxes. 'And did you get those boxes I sent you?'

'Oh, yes,' said Howard.

'Oh good,' said Mr Bullerton. 'And have you finished the work yet?'

'Oh. No,' said Howard.

'Oh dear,' said Mr Bullerton. 'And have you started the work yet?'

'Well, no,' said Howard.

'I see,' said Mr Bullerton, going close. 'Howard Armitage,' he said, **breathing heavily.**

'Hello,' said Howard.

'I do not pay you to sit there saying *"oh".'*

'No,' agreed Howard.

'And I do not pay you to sit there drinking tea.'

'Mm,' agreed Howard.

'I wonder,' said Mr Bullerton, sounding interested, 'what it is you think I do pay you to do?'

'Work,' said Howard. 'Ha ha. Of course.'

'NO!' bellowed Mr Bullerton. **'What I pay you to do is to DO WHAT I TELL YOU TO DO.'**

'Oh! I mean, yes,' said Howard.

'Yes, oh yes,' said Mr Bullerton. 'So just you wait. And in the meantime, I want you to brighten yourself up a bit. Where's your Christmas spirit? Eh?'

'Err…' said Howard. 'I think I used it all up over Christmas.'

'Well GET IT BACK AGAIN,'

shouted Mr Bullerton.

'I'll do my best,' said Howard.

'*Ppffh,*' snorted Mr Bullerton, and left.

'Best be off then,' said the
postman, cheerfully.

'One for the road?' offered
Howard, filling the kettle.

'Ooh, go on then,' said the
postman.

CLATTER! went

the trolley, out in the corridor.
'I'm not standing around here all
day while he guzzles tea. Ten.
Nine.'

'Oh dear,' said Purvis.

'What's it doing?' hissed Mickey
Thompson.

**'FIVE-FOUR-THREE-
TWO-ONE,'** said the trolley.
'RIGHT, I'M OFF.' It gave a
lurch and started to trundle up the
corridor.

'Come on,' said Purvis, hopping
on to the bottom shelf.

'Wait for me!' said Mickey Thompson,

leaping,

and missing.

'Here,' said Purvis, reaching.

'**Yikes**,' said Mickey Thompson, running.

'Hup,' said Purvis, grabbing.

'HELP!

said Mickey Thompson, dangling.

CLATTER!

went the trolley, jerking to a halt.
'You,' it said.

'Meep,' peeped Mickey Thompson.

'If you're getting on, kindly get on. If you're not getting on, kindly get off. One or the other: not both.'

Mickey Thompson got on.

'All aboard, fifty-two?' said the trolley.

'All aboard,' said Purvis, and the trolley clacketty-rattled off up the corridor.

'Phew,' said Mickey Thompson.

'He's a one, isn't he?' whispered Purvis.

'Hmph,' said Mickey Thompson. 'Are you sure about this?'

'Of course,' said Purvis.

'Only we seem to be going quite fast,' said Mickey Thompson.

CRACK! went the trolley, clattering around a corner.

'It's fine,' said Purvis.

CLACK! went the trolley, clattering around another corner.

'PURVIS!' shouted

Mickey Thompson.

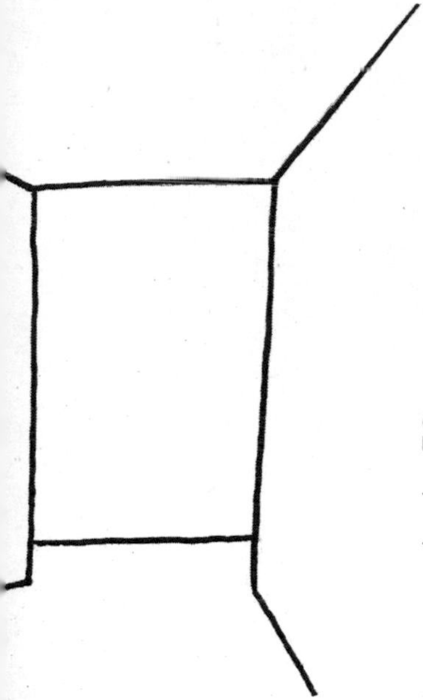

Trolley

'HOLD ON!' **shouted** Purvis.

'THREE TWELVETY TEN!' shouted the trolley, as they barrelled down a corridor.

'NOTHINGY NINE SIX!'

'What's the matter with it?' said Mickey Thompson.

'I think it's over-excited,' said Purvis. 'I'll see if I can have a word.'

He crept to the edge of the shelf and peered out.

'Err, excuse me,' called Purvis. **'SEVENTY MILLIONTY NOTHINGY NOUGHT ONE!'**

'Hello?' called Purvis. **'FIFFERTYFIF FERTYTWOOO**

OOOOOOOOO?'
hooted the trolley.

'Yes, it's me,' said Purvis. 'Err, we were just wondering…'

'WHAT?' shouted the trolley.

'When's the next stop, please?' asked Purvis.

'FIVE TWO FIVE TWO FIVE TWO FIVE TWO FIVE!' shouted the trolley.

Purvis went back in.

'It's no good,' he said. 'He's gone bonkers.'

'What are we going to do?' wailed Mickey Thompson.

'I'm thinking,' said Purvis.

'Think faster,' said Mickey Thompson.

'WHA-OOO!' yelled the trolley, hurtling.

'I'M ON FIRE!'

'*WHAT?!*' *shrieked* Mickey Thompson.

'Oh, shoosh,' said Purvis. 'It's just a figure of speech.'

Trolley

'I think I'm going to be sick,'
said Mickey Thompson.
'DON'T YOU BE
SICK IN ME,'
shouted the
trolley, crashing through some swing doors.

'STAIRS OR LIFT, FIFTY TWO?'

'LIFT!' yelled Purvis.

'HERE WE COME,' shouted the trolley. 'OPEN UP, YOU!'

'PING!' went the lift, just in time. They shot inside and rattled to a halt.

'Well, really,' said the lift.

The mice **plopped** out of the trolley and lay on the lift floor, **puffing.**

'I'm fast, I am,' said the trolley.

'Where's your postman?' said the lift.

'Never mind the postman,' said the trolley.

'Well you didn't ought to go racketing around loose like that,' said the lift. 'You'll cause an accident.'

'Ah, shut up,' said the trolley.

'Ooh, I say,' said the lift. 'Don't you take that tone of voice with me.'

CLATTER! went the trolley.

WHOOSH! went the lift. 'Think you're fast?' it said. 'I'll give you fast.'

'**EEEEEP!**' went the mice.

CLACK!

went the trolley.

WHOOSH! went the lift.

'I think I'm going to be sick,' said Mickey Thompson.

'Oo-err,' said the lift. 'Not in here, lovey, please. See what you've done to him?' it said to the trolley. 'Gone all green, he has.'

'Me?' said the trolley. 'You,

more like; all that **WHOOSH**ing.'

'Whatever were you thinking of, you mice?' said the lift. 'You don't want to go riding about in that clacketty old thing.'

'Oh-ho!' said the trolley. 'Look who's talking!'

'He's bonkers, you know,' whispered the lift.

CLATTER!

went the trolley.

'Err, the thing is,' said Purvis, quickly, 'we wanted to see the not-Christmas tree.'

'Are you sure?' said the lift.

'Yes, please,' said Purvis. 'So could you take us there?'

'YEAH! COME ON!' shouted the trolley. '**TEN. NINE.**'

'Oh leave off, do,' said the lift. 'You're putting me in a tither.'

'**EIGHT. SEVEN,**' shouted the trolley.

'Oo-err,' juddered the lift.

'What is it?' said Purvis.

'He's upset me workings,' said the lift, juddering harder.

'Hold on!'

'OHHHHHH!' shouted everyone as they shot downwards very fast.

'AAAAGGHH!' shouted everyone as they shot upwards very fast.

'EEEEEEEE!'
shouted
everyone
as
they

p
l
u
m
m
e
t
e
d.

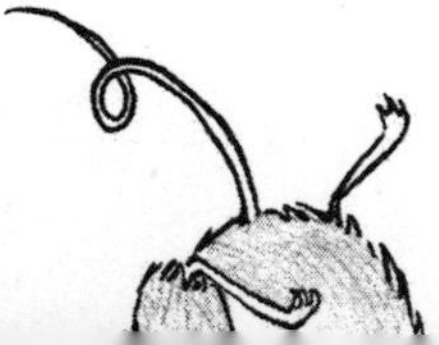

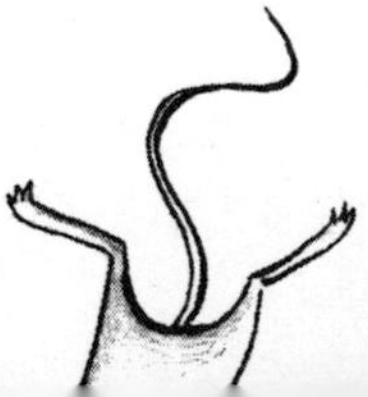

There was a bump, and a ping,
and the mice were

catapulted out of the lift and

'Oo, I say,' called the lift. 'I'm ever so sorry.'

'I'm off,' said the trolley, **clattering** away down a corridor. 'You're dangerous, you are.'

'GET LOST, BONKERS,'

shouted the lift, after it.

'Yeep!' squeaked Mickey Thompson. 'It's a bit sharp.'

'Ye-yeep!' squeaked Purvis, in agreement. 'It's these pine needles.'

'I'm all tangled up,' said Mickey

Thompson, yanking a piece of tinsel.

'Don't squirm,' said Purvis. 'The more you wriggle, the more you'll get spiked.'

'YOUCH,' shouted Mickey Thompson. 'I WANT TO GET OFF.'

'*Shoosh,*' said Purvis. 'Someone'll hear.'

'Good,' said Mickey Thompson. 'Then they can come and unhook me.'

'Yes, and then what?' said Purvis.
'Just hush. I'm trying to think.'

'Think faster,' said Mickey
Thompson.

'What are you doing now?' said
Purvis. 'Stop it.'

'I'm not doing anything,' said
Mickey Thompson.

'Well, what's that swishing
noise?' said Purvis, and they
peered upwards.

'It's a small plastic girl,' said
Mickey Thompson, 'in a huge dress
and wings.'

They watched as the plastic girl
bustled down from branch to branch.

'Hello,'
said Purvis, once
she'd arrived.

'What are you
doing on my
tree?' replied the
girl.

'We're
stuck,' said
Purvis.
'Can you
help?'

'Have you got permission to be on here?' said the girl.

'Err, no,' said Purvis, 'but we weren't expecting…'

'You're not allowed on here without permission,' said the girl. 'It's against the rules.'

'Says who?' said Mickey Thompson.

'Says me,' said the girl, tapping a cardboard badge on the front of her dress. It had the words 'in

charge' written on it in green crayon.

'You made that badge yourself,' said Mickey Thompson.

'No, I didn't,' said the girl, pushing.

'Don't push,' said Mickey Thompson, pushing back. The tree started shaking.

'So what should we do?' Purvis asked the girl, quickly.

'Get off,' said the girl.

'We can't. We're all caught up,' said Purvis. He wriggled to demonstrate and the tree lurched suddenly sideways.

'Oh, I'm going to be sick, I'm

going to be sick,' groaned Mickey
Thompson.

'Not on here you don't,' said
the girl, grabbing him. 'It's against
the rules.

'Can we have a look at these
rules?' asked Purvis.

'No,' said the girl. 'It's against—'

'Please,' said Purvis, 'we could
be stuck on here for ages so—'

'WHAT?' *squawked* the girl
and Mickey Thompson together.

'So if we could read them we'd
know what not to do,' said Purvis.
'Which would mean less trouble
for you.'

'Oh, all *right*,' said the girl.
'Wait here.' She let go of Mickey
Thompson and started to clamber
back up the branches.

'What are you on about?' said
Mickey Thompson. 'We don't want
to read the rules.'

'I know,' giggled Purvis, 'but it
got rid of her, didn't it?'

'No giggling,' said Mickey
Thompson.

'No sicking,' spluttered Purvis.

'Ooh, now you come to
mention it,' said Mickey
Thompson, 'I still
feel…'

PING! went the lift doors opening and Howard came out.

'Howard!' called Purvis. 'Help! We're stuck!'

'SAVE US!' yelled Mickey Thompson, theatrically.

Howard went over to the tree and regarded them.

'Explanation?' he said.

'The trolley upset the lift and we got shot out on to here,' said Purvis. 'We'd only wanted a look. And it's sharp.'

'Yes,' said Mickey Thompson, 'and then a

girl with wings came and told us off and it wasn't even our fault. And I feel sick. And I want to get off.'

'It seems a pity to move you,' said Howard. 'You look so festive.'

'HOWARD!' shouted the mice.

'Yes, yes,' said Howard. 'Give me a chance.'

He found a chair, stood on it, and fumbled about.

'Ouch,' he said.

'I did say,' said Purvis. 'Careful, you're making everything sway.'

'OUCH!' shouted Howard, untangling them, and stuffing them in his pocket.

'Err, Howard,' said Purvis, peeping out.

'Shush,' said Howard.

'Behind you,' *whispered* Purvis.

'Yes, very funny,' said Howard.

'Ah-hem,' said Mr Bullerton.

'*AGH!*' said Howard, falling off the chair.

'Well?' said Mr Bullerton. 'And what is it this time?'

'Ah,' said Howard. 'Hello! I was just having a look at the beautiful tree.'

'And why the chair?' enquired Mr Bullerton.

'I wanted to get very high up,' said Howard, 'and close, so I could... err...'

'Steal the tinsel?' suggested Mr Bullerton.

'No, no,' said Howard, backing towards the lift. 'I wasn't stealing it. I was... err...'

'Do tell,' said Mr Bullerton.

'Smelling it,' said Howard, backing into the lift.

'*What?*' said Mr Bullerton.

'Feeling it,' said Howard,

pressing the button. 'The
Christmas spirit; like you said I
should.'
'COME BACK
HERE,' shouted Mr
Bullerton. 'I…wait.
What's that noise?'

CLATTER! went

the trolley, hurtling into the foyer.
'TIMBER!' hooted the
trolley, bashing into the tree.

went the tree,

toppling

onto Mr

Bullerton.

'ARMITAGE!'

roared Mr Bullerton, as the lift doors shut and Howard and the Clumsies **whooshed** away.

'Phew,' said Howard. 'That was close.'

'Yes, phew,' said Purvis. 'Err, Howard…'

'And he can't blame it on me,' said Howard. 'I wasn't anywhere near that tree when it fell over.'

'No,' said Purvis. 'Err, Howard…'

'What now?' said Howard.

'Too late,' said Purvis.

'I've just been sick in your pocket, Howard,' said Mickey Thompson, cheerfully.

'Oh, marvellous,' said Howard.

POSTCARD

Uncle Gillian

Mickey Thomas & Purvis
An office Somewhere

'They've propped it up again,' said Howard, when he arrived the next morning. 'The tree, I mean.'

'How does it look?' asked Purvis.

'Wonky,' said Howard.

'Oh dear,' said Purvis.

'And scraggy,' said Howard. 'A lot of the needles have fallen off.'

'Gggd,' said Mickey Thompson, shovelling porridge into his mouth.

'Careful,' said Howard. 'I don't want—'

'LOOK OUT!'

shouted Purvis.

'AAGH!' squawked Howard, leaping.

There was a clacketty rattley noise in the corridor and the Clumsies dived under the desk.

'Delivery for Howard Armitage!' announced the postman, coming in with a small envelope.

'What's up, Howard?'

'I thought he was going to be sick again,' said Howard.

'Eh?' said the postman.

'Mic—' coughed Howard. 'Nothing.'

'Mick? Who's Mick?' said the postman.

'No one,' said Howard.

'But you said…'

'TEA?' shouted Howard.

'Best leave it till later,' said the postman, 'what with all the you know what with the thing and the you know who.'

'Quite,' said Howard.

'Still in a fury, he is,' said the postman. 'He said to say have you finished the work in those boxes yet?'

'No,' said Howard. 'I haven't.'

'And did you take something he's lost, or something.'

'No,' said Howard. 'I didn't.'

'Right then,' said the postman, waving the envelope. 'Funny one this: "Care Of" it says.'

'Eh?' said Howard.

'You,' said the postman. 'Care of you, for someone called Purvis. Any ideas?'

'NO!' shouted Howard. 'I'll take it.'

'Long as you're sure,' said the postman, handing it over and leaving.

'What is it?' said Purvis, rushing out.

'Just wait,' said Howard. 'I'm looking.'

'Let me see!' said Purvis. 'It's for me!'

'Care of me,' said Howard. 'Expecting something, were you?'

'No,' said Purvis.

'Hmm,' said Howard. 'Odd.'

He turned the envelope over, and held it up to the light.

'Ouch,' said Howard. 'Stop jabbing.'

'But Howard,' said Purvis.

'Yes, yes, all right,' said
Howard. 'Here, take it.'

Purvis took it, and opened it.

'Oh,' said Purvis.

'Well?' said Howard.

'Err,' said Purvis.

'What does it say?' asked
Mickey Thompson.

'Uncle Gillian's
coming to visit,'
said Purvis.

'Ah,' said Mickey Thompson.

'*Who?*' said Howard.

'Our uncle,' said Purvis.
'Mickey Thompson's, and mine.'

'But what did you say the name was?' said Howard.

'Uncle Gillian,' said Purvis.

'No, no,' said Howard. 'Aunty, surely.'

'No,' said Purvis.

'Or uncle something-or-other-else.'

'No,' said Purvis. 'It's definitely Uncle Gillian.'

'Uncle Gillian,' echoed Mickey Thompson.

'But... surely,' said Howard, rubbing his head. 'And anyway... how...'

'LOOK OUT!' **shouted** Purvis. There was a whizzing noise and something small and round hurtled into the room. It had a big hat and a long scarf and a large bag.

'IT'S ME!'
boomed

Uncle Gillian.

'That was quick,' said Howard.

'So, here we all are,' said Uncle Gillian, looking around. 'Nice elephant.'

'Toot,' went Ortrud, in agreement.

'Kettle, Purvis,' said Uncle Gillian.

'Yes, Uncle Gillian,' said Purvis.

'The room's smaller than I expected,' said Uncle Gillian.

'Excuse me,' said Howard, 'I'm—'

'And what are all these boxes?' said Uncle Gillian.

'Yes, excuse me,' said Howard, 'I'm—'

'And where are the biscuits?' said Uncle Gillian.

'Yes, excuse me,' said Howard. 'I am Howard Armitage, and—'

'Whatty Whatterdidge?' said
Uncle Gillian. 'What kind of a
name is that?'

'It is my name,' said Howard,
'and this is my office.'

'No, no,' said Uncle Gillian.

'Unfortunately, yes,' said
Howard.

'It belongs to my nephews,' said
Uncle Gillian.

'TEA!' **shouted** Purvis.

'No, it doesn't,' said Howard.

'If it's yours as you claim, you
should tidy it up,' said Uncle
Gillian, flinging the bag and hat.

'It's disorganised. What are you doing?' he asked, looking at Howard.

'He's groaning,' said Mickey Thompson.

'Why?' said Uncle Gillian.

'Sometimes he does,' said Mickey Thompson.

'It's not normal,' said Uncle Gillian. 'Hoy. You.'

'Youch,' squawked Howard. 'That hurt.'

'You haven't answered my question,' said Uncle Gillian. 'Where are the—'

'LOOK OUT!' yelled Purvis, and the Clumsies dived under the desk.

'What are you doing?' said Uncle Gillian.

'Hiding,' *whispered* Purvis. 'Quick, come under.'

'No, thanks,' said Uncle Gillian. 'I don't like the look of it.'

'Get under,' hissed Howard.

'I shan't,' said Uncle Gillian. 'You've all taken leave of your senses.'

'GET UNDERNEATH!'

shouted Howard, shoving Uncle
Gillian under the desk just in time
as the door crashed open and
Mr Bullerton

stomped in.

'What?' said Mr Bullerton.

'Hello, Mr Bullerton,' said Howard.

'What did you just shout?' said Mr Bullerton.

'HELLO MR BULLERTON,' shouted

Howard.

'Not that,' tutted Mr Bullerton. 'You were shouting something before the hello Mr Bullerton bit.'

'No, I wasn't,' said Howard.

'Oh, yes you were,' said Mr Bullerton.

'Err, no I wasn't,' said Howard.

'WHAT?' *roared*
Mr Bullerton. 'Don't try
and be funny with me,
matey.'

'No, I wasn't,' said Howard,
'I—'

'This is not a
PANTOMIME.'
'No, Mr Bullerton,' said
Howard.
'It is AN OFFICE.'
'Yes, Mr Bullerton,' said
Howard.
'It is a PLACE OF
WORK,'

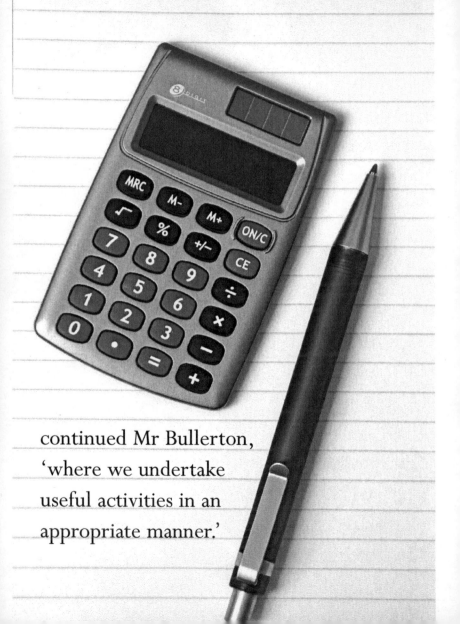

continued Mr Bullerton, 'where we undertake useful activities in an appropriate manner.'

'Indeed it is we do, Mr Bullerton,' said Howard.

'So why were you shouting in an empty room?' said Mr Bullerton.

'Just for the joy of it all,' muttered Howard.

'What?' said Mr Bullerton. 'Speak up.'

'I was just singing a joyful carol,' said Howard.

'Hmm,' said Mr Bullerton, sounding thoughtful.

'Anyway the room wasn't empty,' said Howard. 'I was in it.'

'That amounts to the same thing,' said Mr Bullerton, unpleasantly. 'And you know what else is empty, don't you?'

'No, Mr Bullerton,' said Howard.

'THE TOP OF THE CHRISTMAS TREE,'

bellowed Mr Bullerton.

'Sorry?' said Howard.

'You will be if you don't put that fairy back on sharpish,' said Mr Bullerton.

'But I haven't got it,' said Howard.

'You were on a chair, by the tree, fiddling about,' said Mr Bullerton. 'Don't try and deny it.'

'But I didn't take it,' said Howard.

'PAH,' said Mr Bullerton. 'Put the fairy back where the fairy ought to be or I shall have you arrested.'

'Surely not?' said Howard.

'You've got ONE HOUR,' said

Mr Bullerton,
STOMPING off.

'What are we going to do? What are we going to do?' said Purvis, rushing out and running around in circles.

'I don't know what to do. I don't know what to do,' said

Howard, leaping up and running around in other circles.

'Toot toot. Toot toot,' went Ortrud, joining in.

'If I were you,' said Uncle Gillian, 'I'd put the fairy back, like the man told you to.'

'Oh, YES!' said Howard. 'Oh, what a WONDERFUL idea. Oh, why didn't I think of THAT?'

'Steady on,' said Uncle Gillian.

'Well, how can I put it BACK WHEN I HAVEN'T GOT IT?' **shouted** Howard.

'Hmm,' said Uncle Gillian, narrowing his eyes at Howard.

'What do mean *hmm*?' said Howard.

'It seemed to me the man knew what he was talking about,' said Uncle Gillian, 'and I have to say I found his argument convincing.'

'*AGGHGG GGGHHHHH AGH,*' went Howard.

'Now what's he doing?' said Uncle Gillian.

'Banging the floor with his head,' said Mickey Thompson.

'Don't tell me,' said Uncle Gillian. '*Sometimes he does.*'

'No, it's a new one,' said Mickey Thompson.

'He's upset,' explained Purvis.

'Is he?' said Uncle Gillian. 'Well, we can't have that, can we? Somebody put the kettle on.'

'Please,' croaked Howard. 'Somebody do.'

So Purvis put the kettle on and they all had a cup of tea and calmed down.

'Right then,' said Howard,
draining his cup. 'I'd better go and
see if I can find this wretched tree
ornament.'

'We'll help,' said Purvis.

'Of course we will,' said Uncle Gillian. 'But first we must draw up a plan of action.'

'Why must we?' said Howard.

'So we know what we have to do,' said Uncle Gillian.

'We do know,' said Howard.

'That isn't the point,' said Uncle Gillian.

'There isn't the time,' said Howard.

'Fetch me some paper and a pencil, Purvis,' said Uncle Gillian.

'Fine,' said Howard. 'You do that, and I'll go and find the fairy.'

'Fine,' said Uncle Gillian.

'Fine,' said Howard.

'I thought you'd gone,' said Uncle Gillian.

'**Harrumph,**' said Howard, leaving.

'Good,' said Uncle Gillian. 'Now we can get on. Name?'

'Purvis,' said Purvis.

'Not you,' said Uncle Gillian. 'The fairy.'

'Oh,' said Purvis. 'I don't know.'

'We didn't ask,' said Mickey Thompson.

'That was impolite,' said Uncle Gillian.

'But there wasn't the chance,' said Purvis, 'we—'

'And foolish,' said Uncle Gillian. 'How can we look for something if we don't know what it's called?'

'But we know what she looks like,' said Purvis.

'First things first,' said Uncle Gillian. 'Step one: name the target. We need something catchy and distinctive. Ideas!'

'Err,' said Purvis.

'Um,' said Mickey Thompson.

'Think!' said Uncle Gillian.

'Give me your best.'

'Um,' said Purvis.

'Err,' said Mickey Thompson.

'Tut,' said Uncle Gillian.

'Wait.'

He rummaged in his bag, brought out a newspaper and turned to the back pages.

'Here we are,' he said.

'Banana Tart.'

'Where? Where?' said Mickey Thompson.

'In the 2:50 at Chepstow,' said Uncle Gillian, tapping the paper.

'Oh,' said Mickey Thompson,

disappointedly.

'Don't like it?' said Uncle Gillian. 'How about **Zanzibar Lad?**'

'I'm not sure it's suitable,' said Purvis.

'**Brumpton's Muffler?**' said Uncle Gillian.

'No,' said Mickey Thompson.

'Needs something frillier, you think, for a fairy?' said Uncle Gillian.

'Possibly,' said Purvis.

'She wasn't a real fairy,' said Mickey Thompson. 'I could tell by the wings.'

'So what do you suggest?' said Uncle Gillian.

'Tree Girl,' said Mickey Thompson.

'What girl?' said Uncle Gillian.

'Tree Girl,' said Mickey Thompson.

'I can't tempt you to *Moonlight Melody* in the 3:15?' said Uncle Gillian.

'Tree Girl,' said Mickey Thompson.

'If you must,' sighed Uncle Gillian. 'It's accurate, I suppose, if sadly lacking in romance.'

'That's settled then,' said Purvis.
'And now we'd better get going.'
'Not yet,' said Uncle Gillian.
'Step two: *describe* the target.'
'But Uncle Gillian…' said
Purvis.

'And step two and a half is have another cup of tea,' said Uncle Gillian, 'so stick the

'I'm worried we'll run out of time,' said Purvis, sticking it on.

'We don't want Howard to be arrested, do we?'

'Don't we?' said Uncle Gillian.

'No,' said Purvis, firmly.

'You'd better hurry up with that tea then,' said Uncle Gillian, 'while Mickey Thompson tells me what Tree Girl looks like.'

'There's a face bit and a dress bit and some wing bits at the back,' said Mickey Thompson. 'Pretend ones.'

'Is that the best you can do?' said Uncle Gillian.

'Yes,' said Mickey Thompson.

'Well, it isn't very good,' said
Uncle Gillian.

'Sorry, Uncle Gillian,' said
Mickey Thompson.

'I need to be able to form a
clear image in my mind,' said
Uncle Gillian. 'We'd better build a
replica.'

He disappeared under Howard's
desk and started flinging things out
into the middle of the room.

'Uncle Gillian?' called Purvis,
after a while.

'Enough?' called Uncle Gillian.

'I think so,' called Purvis.

'Then get building,' said Uncle Gillian, emerging.

So Purvis and Mickey Thompson picked through the pile of stuff while Uncle Gillian drank his tea and read the paper.

'The trouble is, none of its very Tree Girly,' said Mickey Thompson, *waving*

a mouldy sausage.

'Mmm, good, good,' said Uncle Gillian, sipping, and flicking.

'He's right, Uncle Gillian,' said Purvis, prodding a sock. 'It isn't.'

'Mmm, yes, yes,' said Uncle Gillian.

Purvis and Mickey Thompson exchanged glances.

'Let's bung any old thing together,' *whispered* Purvis, 'and then go and help Howard.'

'Mmm, yes, yes,' said Mickey Thompson, and after a small scuffle they got **bunging**.

They glued used tissues and
empty crisp packets and old sweet
wrappers on to a cardboard tube,
added bread-wings made from a
leftover sandwich, and glittered
it all.

'I think it's rather striking,' said Purvis, once they'd finished.

'Yes, but what about the face bit?' asked Mickey Thompson.

'What about it?' said Purvis.

'There isn't one,' said Mickey Thompson, 'and there should be: it was in the description I gave.'

'I see,' said Purvis. 'Ooh, I know! The biscuits.'

'Where? Where?' said Mickey Thompson.

'Where? Where?' said Uncle Gillian.

'Here,' said Purvis, fetching the

biscuit tin and rummaging through it. 'Howard's got some smiley face ones. I noticed, earlier.'

'You didn't say,' said Mickey Thompson.

'No. You didn't,' said Uncle Gillian, **narrowing** his eyes.

'I'm saying now,' said Purvis, selecting one.

'But she didn't have a smiley face,' said Mickey Thompson. 'It was cross.'

'We'll stick it on upside down then,' said Purvis, sticking it on upside down. 'How's that?'

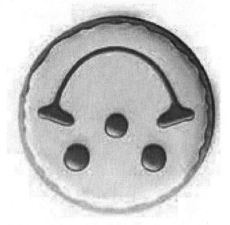

'Ghastly,' said Uncle Gillian.

'It'll just have to do,' said
Purvis. 'Here comes Howard.'

The door opened, closed again
quickly, and opened again slowly.

'**What. Is.** *That?*' said
Howard.

'Tree Girl Two!' announced

Mickey Thompson.

'What girl too?' asked Howard.

'It's the replica fairy,' explained Purvis.

'You're telling me this thing here looks exactly like the missing fairy,' said Howard.

'Well, not actually exactly,' said Purvis.

'Not actually at all,' said Mickey Thompson.

'Well, isn't that just marvellous,' said Howard.

'Yes, isn't it?' said Uncle Gillian. 'I'm delighted to see you've been employing yourselves so usefully while I've been **HUNTING HIGH AND LOW,'** said Howard.

'Glad you appreciate it,' said Uncle Gillian. 'I put a lot of work into that.'

'Oh, did you,' said Howard, 'well… wait… what's that noise?'

There was a loud, high-pitched wailing sound coming from outside.

'Sounds like a siren of some kind,' said Uncle Gillian.

'Toooo000
ooooOOOooot,'

went Ortrud, joining in.

'Help,' **gulped** Howard. 'He must have called them. They're coming for me.'

'Ah, the doctors, is it?' said Uncle Gillian. 'Probably for the best.'

'Not doctors,' squawked Howard. 'Police.'

'So you did steal Tree Girl after all,' said Uncle Gillian. 'I suspected as much.'

Howard lunged at Uncle Gillian and missed. He lunged again, and missed again.

'You didn't tell me he was violent,' called Uncle Gillian, from under the desk.

'He isn't,' called Purvis, back.

'OH YES I AM,' **shouted** Howard.

'There isn't time, Howard,' said Purvis. He grabbed Tree Girl Two, raced into the corridor and gave a loud whistle.

'Wait for me,' yelled Mickey Thompson, racing after him just as there was a clacketty rattley noise and the big wooden post trolley arrived.

'*Eep!*' went Mickey Thompson, hiding.

'WHERE TO, FIFTY TWO?'

said the trolley.

'Tree, please,' said Purvis, hopping on.

'Let's go,' said the trolley, hurtling off.

'WHAT DOES HE THINK HE'S DOING?' **shouted** Howard as the trolley disappeared with Purvis on it.

'HE'S STOLEN MY REPLICA,' **shouted** Uncle Gillian.

'HELP HIM!' **shouted** Mickey Thompson.

'IT ISN'T SAFE!'

So Howard and Mickey Thompson and Ortrud and Uncle Gillian chased up the corridor, around the corner, around the other corner, down the corridor and through the swing doors. In the distance they could see the trolley clattering into the lift, and the lift doors closing.

'STAIRS,' shouted Howard and they bundled down and around and down and around and down into the foyer. There was no sign of the trolley.

'But look,' said Mickey Thompson, pointing upwards. 'It's Purvis, right at the top.'

'*Ouch ouch,*' said
Purvis, carefully positioning Tree
Girl Two on top of the tree.
'There.'

'PURVIS!' **shouted**
Mickey Thompson.

'Hello,' said Purvis, looking
down.

'DON'T LOOK
DOWN,' **shouted**
Howard.

'Ooh, err,' gulped Purvis,
looking up.

'STAY THERE,'

shouted Howard. 'I'LL GO AND FIND THE CHAIR.'

'HELLLLP,'

yelled Purvis, as the tree started swaying, and Tree Girl arrived.

'Hoy,' said Tree Girl.

'What are you doing here?' said Purvis.

'What are *you* doing here?' said Tree Girl.

'We thought you'd been stolen,'

said Purvis.

'I went for a walk,' said Tree Girl.

'Oh!' said Purvis. 'Err… are you allowed to just go off and leave the tree like that?'

'No,' said Tree Girl, 'but I needed a break. Tree duty was supposed to finish weeks ago and it's getting embarrassing: most of the needles have dropped off, and… Hang on a minute. What's this pile of rubbish doing on here?'

'It's a replica of you,' said Purvis. 'We—'

'**Grrr,**'
went Tree Girl.

'No, listen,' said
Purvis, 'I didn't
mean... ***ouch...***
careful.'

'You and it: off,' said
Tree Girl, pushing.

'Wait!' said Purvis.

'***Ouch!*** We were trying
to help. Mr Bullerton said—'

'**HIM,**' **shouted** Tree Girl.

'So he put you up to this, did he?'

'Not exactly,' said Purvis, 'but

when he saw you weren't on the
tree he became enraged and
thought—'

'That's it,' said Tree Girl. 'I've
had enough.'

'Here he comes now,' said
Purvis, as Mr Bullerton and a
policeman came into the foyer.

'This is the scene of the crime,
officer,' said Mr Bullerton,
importantly. 'The fairy used to be
up there.'

'Wasting police time is a very
serious matter, sir,' said the
policeman.

'What?' said Mr Bullerton.

'Look,' said the policeman, pointing, and Mr Bullerton peered upwards. On top of the tree was Tree Girl, just where she should be.

'See?' said the policeman.

'But—' said Mr Bullerton.

'Right,' said Tree Girl, giving the replica a shove.

'*NOOOOO,*' wailed Mr Bullerton, as the replica hurtled towards him, and,

'TAKE THAT!'

shouted Tree Girl, as it thwacked him hard on the head.

THE BIG
SHOW
PART 1

said Howard. 'No,
no, no.'

'No, no what?' asked Purvis.

'I won't, that's what,' said
Howard.

'Won't what?' asked Mickey
Thompson.

'Mm?' said Howard. 'Exactly.

And he can't make me either. I'm putting my foot down. Ouch.'

'You're burbling,' said Uncle Gillian, **whacking** at Howard's shoe. 'Pull yourself together.'

'Yes, isn't it about time you

were going home?' said Howard,
through gritted teeth. 'We wouldn't
want you to outstay your welcome,
would we?'

'Don't you worry about that,'
said Uncle Gillian. 'I can tell when
I'm needed.'

'*No,*' said Howard. '*No, no...*'
'HOWARD,' said Purvis.
'Drink this.' He handed over a cup
of tea, and Howard drank it.

'I needed that,' said Howard.
'Look what Mr Bullerton's just given
me.' He scrumpled the piece of
paper into a ball and hurled it, hard.

Purvis chased it, and un-scrumpled it.

'See what I mean?' said Howard.

'*YOU have been selected to take part in the BIG SHOW,*' read out Purvis.

'**OOOOOH,**' breathed Mickey Thompson.

'*Come'n'Sing. Come'n'Dance. Come'n'Perform,*' continued Purvis.

'**Way-hay!**' cheered Mickey Thompson.

'*Because it's Never Too Late to Celebrate!!!*' finished Purvis.

'Yes, it is,' said Howard. 'It's the middle of January.'

'It'll be great,' said Mickey Thompson, doing a little tap dance. 'What are you going to sing, Howard? What? What?'

'Nothing,' said Howard. 'I won't sing; I won't dance; and I will NOT perform. So there.'

'Won't? Or can't?' said Uncle Gillian, narrowing his eyes at Howard.

'I simply choose not to,' said Howard, huffily.

'I see,' said Uncle Gillian. 'Can't.'

'Oh, leave me alone,' said Howard, slumping.

'Don't worry, Howard,' said Purvis. 'We'll help you.'

'NO!' said Howard. 'Please don't.'

'But Howard…' said Purvis.

'Listen,' said Howard, 'it's very kind of you to offer but I'd really rather prefer it if you didn't interfere.'

'Nonsense,' said Uncle Gillian. 'Of course we'll inter— help. Leave it to me: I have a great deal of experience in the field of theatre.'

'Have you really,' said Howard, through gritted teeth.

'Oh, yes, yes,' said Uncle Gillian. 'I've worked with all the greats, you know.'

'Is that right,' said Howard.

'Oh, yes,' said Uncle Gillian. 'Bernhardt, Olivier…'

'Uh-huh,' said Howard, 'now if you'll excuse me, I've got work to be getting on with.'

He turned to his computer and started **CLATTERING.**

'But Howard,' said Purvis.

'Good bye,' said Howard.

'But Howard,' said Mickey Thompson.

'Go away,' said Howard.

'But—'

'SHOO,' said Howard,

just as everyone disappeared under the desk.

'DON'T YOU SHOO ME,' shouted Mr Bullerton, looming in the doorway.

'*Agh!*' said Howard. 'No I *a-SHOO OOOOOO.*'

'Grrr,' said Mr Bullerton.

'Sorry,' said Howard. 'I've got a spot of hay fever.'

'Don't be absurd,' said Mr Bullerton. 'It isn't the season for hay fever.'

'Isn't it?' said Howard. 'I seem to be losing track of the time.'

'I'll tell you the time,' said Mr Bullerton. 'It's ten past after the time you were supposed to have finished that work I gave you. So where is it?'

'I'm doing it now,' said Howard, starting to **CLATTER** again.

'Stop that,' said Mr Bullerton, 'and pay attention: I've written a song for the show.'

'Oh,' said Howard.

'And...?' said Mr Bullerton, *looming* closer.

'Err… That's nice,' ventured Howard.

'I'm glad you think so,' said Mr Bullerton, 'because you're the one who's going to be singing it.'

Howard GOGGLED at Mr Bullerton.

'Stop GOGGLING,' said Mr Bullerton.

Howard adjusted his expression.

'That's worse,' said Mr Bullerton. 'Try and look normal: there will be a lot of people at the show and I want them to be impressed.'

'Wouldn't it be better if you sang it yourself?' said Howard.

'No,' said Mr Bullerton. 'It wouldn't.'

'Why?' said Howard.

'Because I want you to sing it,' said Mr Bullerton, smirking.

'I can't,' said Howard.

'You will,' said Mr Bullerton.

'But Mr Bullerton,' said Howard, 'we normally have the office show at Christmas time.'

'I cancelled Christmas time,' said Mr Bullerton. 'And if you don't want me to cancel the next

one too you'll work harder. And
faster. And you'll sing when I tell
you to.'

'No, really,' said Howard. 'I
can't sing.'

'Come now,' said Mr Bullerton.
'It was only yesterday I heard you
SINGING A JOYFUL CAROL.'

'So you did,' said Howard.

'And here's your opportunity to
flex those vocal chords again,' said
Mr Bullerton, handing Howard a

folded piece of paper. 'That's my song. Learn it carefully. Practise it hard. Perform it well. Because you don't want to humiliate yourself in front of a vast audience, do you?'

'Not if I can avoid it,' said Howard.

Mr Bullerton made a **Snorting** noise and rushed out of the room.

'**CHOP CHOP,**' said Uncle Gillian, bustling out from under the desk. 'It's time for rehearsals to begin. Pass me that song so we can… ouch.'

'You asked for it,' said Howard.

'I said pass it, not lob it,' said Uncle Gillian. He un-scrumpled the piece of paper and the Clumsies gathered round to read Mr Bullerton's song.

'Howard!' said Purvis.

'What?' said Howard.

'Mmm, yes, yes,' said Uncle Gillian.

'What? What?' said Howard.

'HAR!' spluttered Mickey
Thompson.

'Give it to me,' said Howard,
snatching it up and reading it.

'*I love pretty buttercups*,' read out
Howard.

'*And I love fluffy bunnikins*,' read
out Howard.

'*But best of all I love Mr Buller…*
I'M NOT SINGING
THIS!' shouted Howard.

'Try, Howard,' said Purvis.

'If you don't, he'll sack you,' said Uncle Gillian.

'Oh, all right, ALL RIGHT,' said Howard.

'Good man,' said Uncle Gillian, brandishing a pencil. 'And a-one and two *and*…'

'What are you doing?' said Howard.

'Conducting,' said Uncle Gillian. 'We'll have a quick

run-through before we start
working on it properly. *And…*'

So Uncle Gillian conducted and
Howard sang and Ortrud cantered
about, **trumpeting**. Howard
stopped singing.

'Keep her under control, will you?' he said. 'I can't hear myself properly.'

'Lucky you,' muttered Uncle Gillian.

'What?' said Howard.

'I've got her,' said Purvis, settling Ortrud down. 'Carry on, Howard. You're doing well.'

'Matter of opinion,' muttered Uncle Gillian.

'What?' said Howard.

'*AND...*' **shouted** Uncle Gillian, Jabbing the pencil.

So Howard sang and Uncle

Gillian conducted and the
Clumsies listened attentively.

'There,' *puffed* Howard, once
he'd finished. 'What did you
think?'

'Um, it was quite nice really,'
said Purvis.

'And what's the matter with
him?' said Howard, pointing at
Mickey Thompson.

'He's got something stuck in his
throat,' said Purvis.

'Sorry, Howard,' choked Mickey
Thompson. 'It was great, really it
was.'

'Ever had any voice coaching?' asked Uncle Gillian.

'No,' said Howard.

'I thought not,' said Uncle Gillian.

'Right,' said Howard, 'that's it. There's no way I'm taking part in this show.'

'But it's the BIG show, Howard,' said Mickey Thompson. 'The big one.'

'Nevertheless, I refuse to be made a laughingstock,' said Howard.

'Feeble talk,' said Uncle Gillian.

'You need to put some effort in. Don't just sing the song: feel the song. Let it move you.'

'It moves me all right,' said Howard. 'I'm absolutely furious.'

'GOOD!' shouted Uncle Gillian, springing about.

'Now we're getting somewhere. We'll work with your fury and channel it as a source of creative energy.'

'Can somebody put the kettle on?'

said Howard.

'You must open your heart to the audience,' continued Uncle Gillian, warming to his theme. 'Release your inner voice and then when you step on to that stage and sing, the audience will recognise they're getting the real Howard Armitage.'

'Quite,' said Howard. 'That's what worries me.'

'Now, what are we going to do about the look of you?' said Uncle Gillian.

'What do you mean?' said Howard.

'You can't go on looking like that,' said Uncle Gillian.

'It's the real me,' said Howard.

'It won't do,' said Uncle Gillian.

'I thought you said that's what's

required,' said Howard.

'There are limits,' said Uncle Gillian.

'We could make him a costume,' suggested Purvis.

'I think we'd better,' said Uncle Gillian. 'It'll need to be something that reflects the sentiment of the lyric.'

'The buttercup bit or the bunnikin bit?' asked Mickey Thompson.

'Neither,' said Howard.

'How about some furry trousers?' suggested Mickey Thompson.

'You can stop right there,' said Howard.

'Yes, we don't want to be too literal,' said Uncle Gillian. 'The song isn't really about buttercups or bunnikins. It's about love. That's the aspect we need to draw out.'

'I thought we'd settled on fury,' said Howard.

'Furious love,' said Uncle Gillian.

'Love and fury intertwined.'

'I'd prefer to stick with pure fury,' said Howard.

'Tough,' said Uncle Gillian.

'**Grr,**' said Howard.

'I'll see what I can find under the desk,' said Purvis, disappearing.

'No, don't,' said Howard.

'Yes, do,' countered Uncle Gillian. 'There's about a **ton** of rubbish under it so there's bound to be something suitable.'

'Oh, thank you very much,' said Howard.

'Pleasure,' said Uncle Gillian.

'Now sing it again while we're waiting. *AND*...'

So Uncle Gillian conducted and the mice rummaged while Howard sang and

Ortrud curled up in a

ball with her trunk over her ears.

Suddenly there was a great
C L A C K I N G and
R A T T L I N G in the corridor.
Howard only just had time to
chuck his coat over Uncle Gillian
and Ortrud before the postman
came running in.

'WHAT IS IT?
WHAT'S WRONG,
WHAT?' he **shouted.**

'*#fff?*' **puffed** Howard,
trying to look relaxed.

'Why were you screaming?' said
the postman.

'I was not screaming,' said
Howard. 'I was singing.'

'Are you sure?' said the postman.

'I should know,' said Howard. 'I was rehearsing for that… thing.'

'The Big Show?' asked the postman.

'I believe that's what they're calling it this year,' said Howard.

'I wouldn't have thought it would be your cup of tea, Howard,' said the postman. 'Speaking of which—'

'No time, unfortunately,' said Howard. 'I've got an awful lot of rehearsing to do if I'm ever going to be ready.'

'You can say that again,' giggled the postman. 'You don't want to humiliate yourself in front of a vast audience, do you, Howard?'

'Harrumph,' said Howard.

'Here's your post then,' said the postman, waving a funny-shaped package. 'It's another of those care-ofs you've been getting lately.'

'What?' said Howard.

'This one's care of you for someone called MISE.'

'I don't want it,' said Howard, backing away.

'I'll put it on the desk,' said the postman. 'Are you sure you're all right?'

'**Ugh,**' said Howard.

'And good luck with the show. I'll come along and watch.'

'**Ugh,**' said Howard.

The postman left the room and the mice charged out from under the desk.

'What have we got?' they said as they raced up on to the desk and over to the package.

'If it's anything like the last one, nothing but trouble,' said Howard,

as they ripped the package open
and something rolled out.
'TREE GIRL!'
shouted Mickey Thompson.

'What's that thing doing here?'
said Howard.

'What are you doing here?'
Purvis asked Tree Girl.

'I've come to visit,' said Tree
Girl.

'Tree Girl's come to visit,
Howard,' said Mickey Thompson.

'Get rid of it,' said Howard.

'But Howard—' said Purvis.

'If Mr Bullerton finds it here

he'll think I've stolen it,' said
Howard.

'I'm going nowhere,' said Tree
Girl, fluffing her wings. 'I'm sick
of being stuck on that tree. It isn't
even Christmas time any more. It's
against the rules to have a Christmas
tree when it isn't Christmas time.'

'Is it?' said Purvis.

'Clue's in the name,' said Tree
Girl, winking.

'Tree Girl says she's going
nowhere, Howard,' said Mickey
Thompson.

Howard started pacing up and
down.

'Why me?' he said. 'Why?'

'I'll put the kettle on,' said Purvis.

'That elephant and the mice were bad enough without the Gillian one and now there's this thing too,' said Howard, still pacing. 'It isn't right.'

'Don't worry, Howard,' said Purvis.

'I don't see what he's got to worry about,' said Tree Girl. 'He doesn't have to spend all day with a tree up his skirt.'

'He usually wears trousers,' said Mickey Thompson.

'I wish you'd stop talking about my trousers,' said Howard. 'My trousers have nothing to do with anything.'

'I wanted him to wear furry ones for his song costume,' explained Mickey Thompson. 'But we couldn't find anything furry under the desk except a mouldy sausage.'

'I can get you some tinsel if you like,' said Tree Girl.

'Yes, please,' said Purvis. 'Although I don't know whether Howard and Uncle Gillian—'

'Where is Uncle Gillian?' said
Mickey Thompson.

'Is that him?' said Tree Girl,
pointing to a kerfuffle going on
under Howard's coat.

'*Gerroff... get... out,*' said
Uncle Gillian, thrashing around.

'**Toooot!**' went Ortud, in alarm.

'This is outrageous,' said Uncle
Gillian, wriggling free.

'Oh dear, did you get stuck?' said
Howard. 'What a pity.'

'How would you like it if
someone covered you in an
enormous coat and left you there?'

demanded Uncle Gillian.

'I'd like it very much indeed,' said Howard. 'In fact, it's an excellent idea.'

He picked up the coat, flung it over his head, and lay down under the desk.

'Err, Howard,' said Mickey Thompson.

'This is no time for a nap,' said Uncle Gillian. 'We haven't finished rehearsing.'

'I'm not doing it,' said Howard, muffledly. 'I've gone away.'

'What are we going to do now?'

wailed Purvis. 'If he doesn't sing in the show he'll get fired.'

'And if he does sing in the show he's going to humiliate himself in front of a vast audience,' said Uncle Gillian. 'I tried my best with him but there's only so much one can do when faced with a fundamental lack of talent. I haven't got a magic wand to wave, you know.'

'I have,' said Tree Girl, waving it.

'Careful,' said Uncle Gillian, ducking.

'It isn't a real magic wand,' said Mickey Thompson.

'Yes, it is,' said Tree Girl.

'I don't believe you,' said Mickey Thompson. *'Ouch!* Don't do that with it.'

'We've got to help him somehow,' said Purvis. 'What would you have to do to magic him, Tree Girl?'

'I'm not really supposed to say,' said Tree Girl.

'Can you give us a rough idea?' asked Purvis. 'Then we could see if it's feasible.'

'OK,' said Tree Girl. 'Hypothetically speaking, I'd fly around his head fifteen to twenty times waving the wand and shouting *SING WELL, SING WELL,* or something along those lines.'

'I see,' said Purvis.

'We'd tweak the words, of course,' said Tree Girl.

'In what way?' asked Purvis.

'Make them more poetic,' said Tree Girl. 'And add in any extras.'

'Such as?' said Purvis.

'It'd be up to you,' said Tree Girl. 'You could have "*sing well and*

extremely loudly," for example, or
"*sing well with a nimble dance*".'

'Could he do a little tap
routine?' asked Mickey Thompson.

'If you want,' said Tree Girl.

'That's settled then,' said Purvis.

'There's one slight problem,'
said Tree Girl.

'What's that?' asked Purvis.

'My wings aren't working,' said
Tree Girl.

'I said so, didn't I?' whispered
Mickey Thompson, to Purvis.

'Eh?' whispered Purvis.

'Pretend Ones,' mouthed

172

Mickey Thompson.

'Not pretend; substitute,' said
Tree Girl. 'My other ones are
being repaired. The mechanism
kept **sticking**.'

'Hmm,' said Purvis. 'How
would it be if you waved the wand
from wherever you happened to
be standing?'

'It wouldn't work,' said Tree
Girl. 'I need to get some speed up.'

'There's a simple solution,' said
Uncle Gillian. 'We attach her to a
piece of string and *whisk*
her around the top of his head.'

'How would you feel about that, Tree Girl?' asked Purvis.

'I'll give it a go,' she said.

So they tied a piece of string around Tree Girl and trooped over to Howard, who was snoring under the desk.

'It's logistically tricky,' said Uncle Gillian, pulling the coat away from Howard's head. 'I think we'll have to climb on to his face and launch her from there.'

Everyone started to climb.

'Hang on a minute,' said Uncle Gillian.

Everyone stopped climbing.

'I think it would be better if Ortrud waited on the floor,' said Uncle Gillian.

So Ortrud sat on the floor and watched while everyone else

climbed up the side of Howard and on to his face. He was still snoring heavily as Tree Girl got into position.

'Get ready,' said Uncle Gillian, grasping Tree Girl's string.

'Good luck!' said Purvis, passing Tree Girl's wand.

'Oink oink,' said Mickey Thompson, tickling Howard's nose.

'FWAGHAH!'

sneezed Howard, jerking suddenly upright and cracking his head on the desk as all the mice and Tree Girl tumbled down around him.

The Big
Show
Part 2

'FWAGHAH!'

Howard sneezed again. He rolled out from under the desk and lay on the floor, groaning.

'LOUDSINGFASTDANCE,'

shouted Tree Girl, launching herself at Howard's head and bashing him with the wand.

'Oof,' said Howard, passing out.

'That wasn't particularly poetic,' said Uncle Gillian, to Tree Girl.

'It was the best I could manage under the circumstances,' said Tree Girl.

'Do you think it'll be enough?' asked Purvis.

'I've no idea,' said Tree Girl. 'I don't normally work this way. It's most irregular.'

'Sorry, Tree Girl,' said Purvis.

'And you shouldn't have oinked him,' said Uncle Gillian, to Mickey Thompson.

'Sorry, Uncle Gillian,' said Mickey Thompson.

'What shall we do?' asked Purvis. 'Should we call a doctor, do you think?'

'Let's try this first,' said Uncle Gillian. He picked up a cup of cold tea and emptied it over Howard.

'*Phwphwphwer,*' said Howard.

'That's better,' said Uncle Gillian.

180

'What happened?' spluttered Howard.

'It's entirely your own fault,' said Uncle Gillian. 'You shouldn't have been under there. Silly place to sleep, in my opinion.'

'Who are you?' said Howard.

'Uncle Gillian,' said Uncle Gillian.

'Who?' said Howard.

'Uncle Gillian,' said Uncle Gillian.

'Aunty, surely,' said Howard.

'Would you like a cup of tea?' said Purvis, quickly.

'He's only just had one,' giggled Mickey Thompson.

'Yuck,' said Howard. 'I don't want tea. I hate tea.'

Ortrud **trumpeted** and the mice **gasped**.

'What are you looking at me like that for?' said Howard.

'Nothing, nothing,' said Uncle Gillian. 'But now you're awake we ought to be cracking on. There isn't much time left.'

'Until what?' said Howard.

'The Big Show!' said Mickey Thompson.

'Ooooh,' breathed Howard.
'Are we going to go and watch?'
'You'll be doing more than
that,' said Uncle Gillian.
'Eh?' said Howard.
Purvis found the flyer
and handed it to Howard.

'*YOU have been selected to take
part...*' read out Howard.

'*Come'n'Sing. Come'n'Dance.
Come'n'...*'

'Me?' said Howard.
'Yes,' said everyone.
'Really?' said Howard.
'Yes,' said everyone.

'**WAY-HAY!**'

cheered Howard. 'I love performing.'

'But Howard…' said Purvis.

'Why are you looking so serious?' said Howard, leaping up and doing a little tap dance. 'It's never too late to celebrate, you know!'

Purvis and Mickey Thompson exchanged glances.

'GONE BONKERS,' mouthed Mickey Thompson.

'But what am I going to wear?' said Howard, swivelling his hips. 'I'll need to get a costume sorted out.'

'Well…' began Purvis.

'What's my look, man?' said Howard, swivelling harder.

'Yes, err, we were thinking about that earlier,' said Purvis. 'Tree Girl said she could get us some tinsel but I wasn't sure whether you'd—'

'BRILLIANT!'

shouted Howard. 'I likes her style.
Get lots. And some silver foil. I
wanna razzle-dazzle 'em.'

'Just hold on a minute,' said
Uncle Gilllian. 'I'm not sure tinsel
and silver foil are very
appropriate.'

'Don't be a square, daddio,' said
Howard, pirouetting. *Wheee!'*

'Well, really,' tutted Uncle
Gillian, dodging out of the way
just in time. 'I believe we'd agreed
the costume should reflect and

enhance the message of the song.'

'What song?' said Howard.
'What message?'

'Do you really not remember?' asked Purvis.

'How do you think I should have my hair?' said Howard.

'Listen,' said Uncle Gillian.
'Mr Bullerton has written a song especially for you to sing at the show.'

'NO!' shrieked Howard.

'Yes,' said Uncle Gillian.

'Here,' said Purvis, handing it to Howard.

'*I love pretty buttercups*,' read out Howard.

'*And I love fluffy bunnikins*,' read out Howard.

'*But best of all I love Mr Buller…* I'M NOT SINGING THIS!' **shouted** Howard. 'IT DOESN'T EVEN RHYME.'

'But Howard—' said Purvis.

'I am an ARTIST,' **shouted** Howard.

'Yes but Howard—' said Mickey Thompson.

'If Bullerton wants me to sing I'll SING,' shouted Howard, 'but it won't be this twaddle.'

'What'll it be then?' said Uncle Gillian.

'"GREAT BALLS OF FIRE",' ROARED Howard, leaping, and doing the splits. 'Oh, yessssss.'

'WHOO-HOO!' cheered Mickey Thompson.

'Oh dear,' said Purvis.

'Help me up,' said Howard.

'We'd better have a quick run-
through,' said Uncle Gillian, as
they helped Howard up. 'And a
one and two *and*…'

So Howard sang 'Great Balls of
Fire' while Uncle Gillian
conducted and the others listened.

'TA-DA,' *puffed* Howard,
once he'd finished. 'What did you
think?'

'Um…' said Purvis.

'I've never heard anything like
it,' muttered Uncle Gillian.

'Neither have I,' said Howard.
'They're going to love me. How

long have we got until the show
starts?'

'About an hour,' said Purvis.

'That's loads of time,' said
Howard.

'Only if we concentrate,' said
Uncle Gillian. 'And a one and two
and…'

'What are you doing?' said
Howard.

'Rehearsing,' said Uncle Gillian.

'We've just done that,' said
Howard.

'And we'll keep doing it until
you improve,' said Uncle Gillian.

'You can't improve on perfection, sweetie,' said Howard, cart-wheeling out of the door. 'I'm popping out.'

'Howard!' called Purvis. 'You can't! You're not ready.'

'Laters, gators,' called Howard, back.

Everyone looked at each other.

'What are we going to do now?' groaned Purvis. 'He's even worse than he was before.'

'I agree,' said Uncle Gillian. 'He should have stuck with the buttercups.'

'I prefer "Great Balls of Fire", as a song,' said Mickey Thompson.

'As a song, yes,' said Uncle Gillian, 'but not when it's sung by him. It's way beyond his vocal capabilities. Even the elephant makes a nicer noise.'

Ortrud **tooted** in agreement.

'May I make a suggestion?' said Tree Girl.

'As long as you watch what you're doing with that wand,' said Uncle Gillian, moving further away.

'Well,' said Tree Girl, 'if we put a lot of effort into the costume and make it really spectacular, it might take the audience's mind off the singing.'

'It would have to be very spectacular indeed,' said Uncle Gillian.

'Maybe we should add spectacular special effects,' suggested Mickey Thompson.

'I could do you some flames,' offered Tree Girl. 'They'd go nicely with the words.'

'No,' said Uncle Gillian.

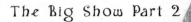

'I've got a better idea.'

He grabbed the pot of glitter they'd used for the replica and took the lid off one of Howard's boxes of work.

'Err, Uncle Gillian,' said Purvis. 'I don't think you ought to—'

'Do you want to help him or not?' said Uncle Gillian.

'Yes,' said Purvis. 'Of course, but—'

'Well then,' said Uncle Gillian. 'Scissors.' He held out his hand and Mickey Thompson handed him the scissors.

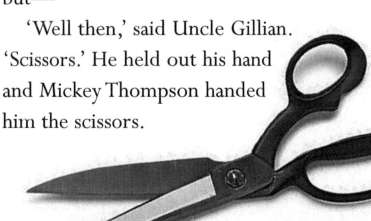

'Glue,' said Uncle Gillian.
Purvis handed him the glue. There
was a lot of cutting and squirting
and sprinkling and then Uncle
Gillian flung a large handful of
something up in the air.

'There,' he said. 'Special effects.'

'Ooooo!' said everyone else, as
hundreds of pieces of glittery
confetti fluttered down. **'Lovely!'**

'Come on then,' said Purvis.
'There isn't much time left.'

So everyone rushed around in a
panic finding the tinsel and the
silver foil and making confetti.

Then everyone sat around in a panic waiting for Howard to come back.

'Where is he? Where is he?' said Purvis.

'It's most unprofessional of him to disappear like this,' said Uncle Gillian.

'Maybe he's run off,' said Mickey Thompson, just as the door flew open and Howard pirouetted in.

'Whee!' said Howard. 'Look who's here.'

'DOG!' shouted Uncle Gillian.

'ALLEN!' shouted the mice, running over to Allen. 'I've brought him to see the show,' said Howard. 'I knew he wouldn't want to miss my performance.'

'Mr Bullerton won't be very pleased,' said Purvis.

'Good,' said Howard. 'Now

everyone stand back while I
practise my moves.'

Everyone stood back while
Howard practised his moves.

'He doesn't seem himself,' said
Allen, worriedly.

'He got bonked on the head,'
explained Purvis. 'Twice.'

'Oh dear,' said Allen.

'And Tree Girl magicked him,'
said Mickey Thompson.

'Oh no,' said Allen.

'CAREFUL!' **shouted**
Uncle Gillian, as Howard went
spinning past. 'He's out of control.

We've got to stop him and get him into his outfit or we won't make curtain-up.'

'HOWARD!' shouted Purvis, trying to flag him down. Howard continued spinning.

'HOWARD!' shouted Mickey Thompson. 'Look at the pretty tinsel.'

Howard spun faster.

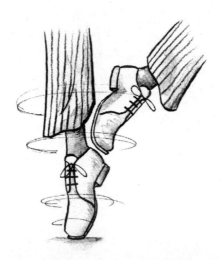

'Help me with this,' said Uncle
Gillian, pushing a box into the
middle of the room.

'Why are we pushing it?' asked
Purvis.

'Oops,' said Howard, tripping
over it, and crashing to the
ground.

'That's why,' said Uncle Gillian.
'Come and sit on him, Ortrud.'
Ortrud went and sat on him.

'Oof,' said Howard.

'Now help me with the
costume,' said Uncle Gillian. They
put the silver foil over him, wound

the tinsel up and down him and
tied it, *tightly*.

'Um…' said Allen.

'I do wish he'd keep still,' said
Uncle Gillian, stapling on some
sweet wrappers.

'Excuse me,' said Allen.

'What's up, Allen?' asked Purvis.

'He's gone a little bit purple,' said Allen.

They loosened the tinsel.

'That's better,' said Allen.

'Are we ready then?' asked Purvis.

Howard made a croaky noise.

'I think he's trying to say something,' said Allen.

'What is it, Howard?' asked Purvis.

'My head,' groaned Howard.

'He's right,' said Mickey Thompson. 'It needs a little something extra.'

'There's no time to make a hat, or wig,' said Uncle Gillian.

'Glitter him,' said Tree Girl. So they squirted glue over Howard's head and...

glittered him.

'*Phpp, phpp,*' said
Howard, s p i t t i n g bits out.

'A definite improvement,'
said Uncle Gillian. 'Now how
are we going to get him
there?'

'I know!' said Purvis. He
raced into the corridor, gave
a loud whistle, and with a
deafening clacketty-rattle the
big wooden post trolley
arrived.

'What's that?' said the
trolley, looking at Howard.

'It's Howard,' said Purvis.

'We need to get him to the Big Show, fast.'

'Pop him on, then,' said the trolley.

With some difficulty, the Clumsies and Allen and Uncle Gillian and Tree Girl heaved Howard upright and manoeuvred him over to the trolley.

'Maybe we shouldn't have wrapped him up so much,' said Purvis.

'We had to, really,' said Mickey Thompson, 'otherwise he'd still be spinning.'

'True,' said Purvis.

'Hurry up,' said the trolley, so they laid Howard across the top, stacked the boxes of confetti underneath, and climbed on. **CRACK,** went the trolley. **'ALL ABOARD, FIFTY TWO?'**

'All aboard,' said Purvis, and they shot off up the corridor.

'AAAAAAAGGG GHHHHHHHH!' shouted everyone as they swerved

around corners

and crashed through doors and
hurtled along passageways they'd
never hurtled along before.

'VROOM,'

ROARED the trolley, turning sharp left and plunging into a tunnel.

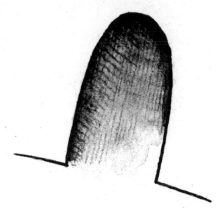

'**TOOT!**' went Ortrud.

'I can't see!' said Allen.

'Head,' said Howard.

'Hold on!' said Purvis.

'I feel sick!' said Mickey
Thompson.

'It isn't allowed!' said Tree Girl.

'I want to go home!' said Uncle
Gillian.

'**YEE-HI**,' whooped the trolley,
bursting them into brightness
again and skidding to a halt. 'Fast.'

'We're here,' said Purvis,
blinking.

And there they were by the side

210

of a stage, with hot lights above it
and a vast audience in front of it.

'Wow,' gulped Mickey
Thompson. 'Look at them all.'

Suddenly there was a **LOUD**
drum-roll and Mr Bullerton
strutted on to the stage.

'Ladies and Gentlemen,' he said.
'Welcome to the Big Show, and for
our first act tonight we have a
very, er... interesting singer-
songwriter who has written a song
all by himself especially for you.'

'Oo!' said the audience.

'Aah!' said Allen. 'That's nice. I
wonder who it is?'

211

'Hang on a minute,' said Mickey Thompson.

'Dastardly,' said Uncle Gillian. 'The man's a scoundrel.'

'And so, Gentlemen and Ladies,' continued Mr Bullerton, 'please put your hands together and give a very warm welcome to **HOWARD ARMITAGE** and his song *Buttercups*, written entirely and exclusively just by him.'

The audience clapped politely as Mr Bullerton left the stage, and then there was silence.

'Here we go,' said Uncle Gillian. 'Time for "Great Balls of Fire".'

'But where is he?' said Purvis,

looking around.

'He must have rolled off,' said the trolley. 'I thought I heard a bump, in the tunnel.'

'Look,' said Mickey Thompson. 'Mr Bullerton's coming back on.'

'Err, Ladies and Gentlemen,' said Mr Bullerton. 'Unfortunately it would appear that Howard Armitage cannot be with us tonight.'

The audience made surprised-and-disappointed noises.

'However,' said Mr Bullerton, 'I'm determined that you hear the

214

words of the song so I'm going to read them out to you, and very memorable I think you'll find them. Ah-hem.' He cleared his throat and took a piece of paper out of his pocket.

'Quick!' said Uncle Gillian.
'Bring the curtain down!'

'Yes, but how?' said Purvis.

'It'll be one of those,' said
Uncle Gillian, pointing at a row of
coloured buttons just as Howard
arrived, dishevelledly.

'I fell off,' he said, as Mr
Bullerton began to read.

'*I love pretty buttercups,*' read out
Mr Bullerton.

'*And I love fluffy bunnikens.*'

The audience tittered, and
Purvis pressed the green button.
Nothing happened.

'*But most of all*,' continued Mr
Bullerton, '*I love*… **HOWARD
ARMITAGE!**' he roared, as
Howard staggered on to the stage,
trailing tinsel.

The audience gasped.

'Give it to me,' said Howard,
grabbing the microphone.
'*Give it to
ME*,' **shouted** Mr Bullerton,
grabbing it back.

'**ME,**' **shouted** Howard, wrestling it free and capering off with it down to the front of the stage.

'GOODNESS GRACIOUS,' whooped Howard. 'GREAT BALLS OF FIRE!' He started swivelling, and someone in the audience screamed.

'AAAAAA ARMMMMI IITAAAAGE

!!!!!!!!!' roared

Mr Bullerton.

'Oh, no,' said Uncle Gillian.
'Somebody make him stop.'

Purvis
pressed the
red button
and the
fire alarm
went off.
Allen jabbed
the blue button and jets of water
squirted out of the ceiling. Mickey
Thompson bashed the yellow

button and a wind-machine blew
the lids off the boxes and scattered
the confetti. Uncle Gillian hit the
purple button and a light fell from
the ceiling and crashed on to
Howard. Howard stopped
swivelling.

'Ouch,' he said.

'AAAAAAA
RMMMMIII
TAAAAGE!!!
!!!!!' roared
Mr Bullerton, again.

'Where am I?' said Howard.
'What's happening?'

'You're FIRED,'
shouted Mr Bullerton. 'That's
what's happening.'

He lunged at Howard, and
missed. He lunged again and
missed again, and the audience
started shrieking and running
about.

'Somebody help him,' wailed
Allen.

'FLING ME,' shouted
Tree Girl. **'FLING ME'**.

So Ortrud picked up Tree Girl

in her trunk and flung her, and the wind machine whisked her up and up and around and around and dropped her on Mr Bullerton's head.

'Ouch,' said Mr Bullerton. '**DEEP SLEEP LOUD SNORE,**' **shouted** Tree Girl, whacking him with the wand.

'**Oof,**' said Mr Bullerton,
passing out.

'Magic,' said Tree Girl.

'Gosh,' said Mickey Thompson.

'Why am I covered in tinsel?'
said Howard. 'And why are those
people shrieking?'

'Mmm, yes,' said Uncle Gillian.
'A good performer knows when
it's time to make an exit, and that
time is now.'

'He's right,' said the trolley.
'Climb on, everyone.' Everyone
climbed on.

'**ALL ABOARD, FIFTY
TWO?**' said the trolley.

'All aboard!' said Purvis.

'Then let's get out of here, FAST,' said the trolley, and with an enormous CLATTER they did.